THE THREE LITTLE PIGS

RETOLD BY
MARIAN HARRIS

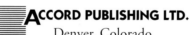

ILLUSTRATED BY
JIM HARRIS

ACCORD PUBLISHING LTD.
Denver, Colorado

No part of this book may be reproduced or transmitted in any form or by any means, electronic or mechanical, including photocopy, recording, or any information storage and retrieval system, without permission in writing from the publisher. For information address Accord Publishing Ltd, 1407 Larimer Square, Suite 206, Denver, CO 80202

Designed by Heather Stilb Fleck

FIRST EDITION
ISBN 0-939251-57-4

Library of Congress Cataloging-in-Publication Data
Harris, Marian, 1961-
The three little pigs / retold by Marian Harris;
illustrated by Jim Harris. —1st ed.
p.   cm.
Summary: Retells the adventures of three little pigs, two brothers and their sister, as they leave home to seek their fortunes and try to evade the big bad wolf.
ISBN 0-939251-57-4 (hardcover)
[1. Folklore.   2. Pigs—Folklore.]
I. Harris, Jim, 1955- ill. II. Three little pigs. English. III. Title.
PZ8.1.H24Th 1995
398.24'529734—dc20
[E]   95-20593
                                               CIP
                                               AC

Printed in Hong Kong

Dedicated to wonderful grandfathers like
Bapa, Papa, and Opa

O nce upon a time there were three little pigs who lived with
their mother at the edge of the forest.

Early one morning they were eating breakfast, when the
mother pig began to cry.

"Oh, my," she sniffed, "you little piglets…why, look at
you…you're all grown up! It's time for you to make your own
homes."

"Hurrah!" squealed the first little pig. "No more chores!"

"Yippee! Mudbaths every day!" shouted the second little pig.

"At last!" squealed the third little pig. "A room of my very own!"

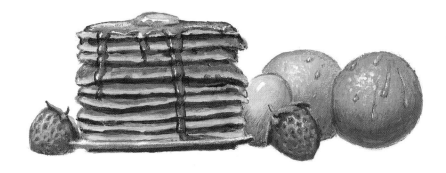

The mother pig dabbed her eyes. "But what if you meet the Big Bad Wolf?"

"Awwwwww, who's afraid of a Big Bad WOLF?" giggled the first little pig.

"Not me!" snickered the second little pig.

But the third little pig had seen the wolf when he was digging for truffles in the forest. He remembered sharp, yellow teeth and a long, red tongue. "Don't worry," he said, "we'll be *very* careful."

So the mother pig packed them each a snack—7 loaves of crispy French bread, 19 cheese biscuits, 14 blackberry jelly rolls, 15 saltwater taffies, 4 blueberry pies, 8 chocolate éclairs, and 592 roasted chestnuts—and kissed them good-bye on their rubbery, red noses.

The first little pig meandered along the hawthorn hedge munching saltwater taffy 'til he came to a farmer pitching straw onto a wagon. It made the pig tired just watching. He thought how nice it would be to have a place to stretch out his bedroll.

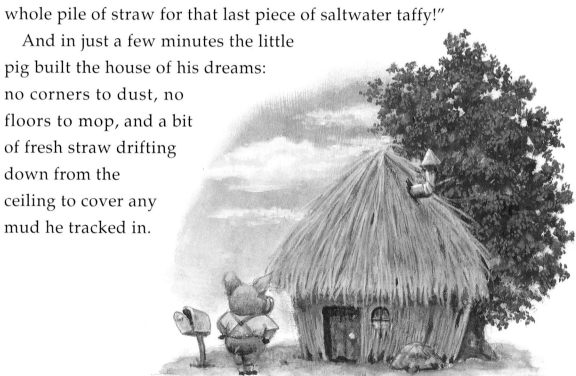

"May I have some straw to build a house?"
he asked.

"Why, yes," chuckled the farmer. "I'll trade you a
whole pile of straw for that last piece of saltwater taffy!"

And in just a few minutes the little
pig built the house of his dreams:
no corners to dust, no
floors to mop, and a bit
of fresh straw drifting
down from the
ceiling to cover any
mud he tracked in.

He was stretching out for a well-deserved snooze when a sly
voice whispered, "Liiiiittle piiiiig, liiiiittle piiiiig. Let me come in!"
Through a crack the little pig spied a long, gray tail.
"Not by the hair of my chinny-chin-chin!" he squeaked.

"Then I'll huff, and I'll puff, and I'll BLOW your house in!" growled the wolf.

But it only took one HUFFFFFFFF! And with that, the wolf was so busy shaking straw out of his ears that all he could see was a curly, white tail wriggling away beneath the hawthorn hedge.

Meanwhile, the second little pig crossed a beaver dam and met a man with a load of sticks. "Could I have some sticks to build a house of my own?" she asked, stuffing a handful of chestnuts into her full mouth.

"Certainly," replied the man, "if you'll share a few of those chestnuts."

And before you could say, "Lifferty, Lafferty, my son Rafferty," the little pig had built her very own stick house—right next to a beautiful, black mudhole, of course.

Suddenly the first little pig scampered up. "The w-w-wolf," he wailed, " b-b-blew down my house!"

"Hee hee hee!" giggled the second little pig, "I'm not afraid of a wolf. Relax and take a dip with me!"

Before long the pigs were sleepy. But they had
no sooner hung the second pig's hammock when...
RAP! RAP!

The pigs peered through the keyhole. All
they could see were claws. LOTS of claws.

"Little pigsssss, let me come in," snarled a
nasty voice, "or I'll huff, and I'll puff, and I'll BLOW your house in!"

"Not by the hair of my chinny-chin-chin!" croaked the second little pig.

So the wolf huffed. And sticks blew off the roof. He huffed again. And the stick door blew off one of its hinges. Then, he PUFFED. And the whole stick house fell sideways into the beautiful, black mudhole.

But by the time he wiped the mud off his face, all the wolf could see were two curly tails bounding across the beaver dam.

Now the third little pig was sitting beside a stream eating his mother's blueberry pies when a man came along, pushing a cart piled high with bricks.

"Have a seat," invited the third little pig, and he gave the man a piece of pie.

"Why, thank you," said the man. "This is delicious."

The little pig took a bite of pie, too. "May I please have some bricks to build a house?" he asked.

The man shook his head sadly, "If I don't sell these bricks at market, I'll have no money to buy food for my family."

The third little pig nodded. He remembered digging for truffles in the forest and selling them every Saturday morning—one for a penny, twelve for a dime. It had taken weeks to fill his piggy bank. Then he remembered the Big Bad Wolf.

"I'll trade you my piggy bank for the bricks," he said softly.

The man shook the heavy piggy bank. "I declare!" he exclaimed. "This'll buy potatoes and beans to feed my children all winter!" So the man walked away with the piggy bank and the pig trundled off with the bricks.

Heave and haul. Push and pour. All day the third little pig worked, building a magnificent brick house with carved wooden shutters, a white picket fence, and a bedroom of his very own.

He was painting the mailbox when his brother and sister rushed out of the woods. "Help!" they squealed, "the WOLF!"

Quick as a flash, the third little pig grabbed their black hooves, pulled them into his sturdy house, and slammed the door.

"You poor piglets," he murmured when he heard their sad stories. "I believe you could use some cinnamon tea."

CrrreeeeaakkkKKK! Somebody opened the picket gate.

"Little pigs, little pigs, let me come in," snarled a dark, growly voice.

The first two pigs shivered.

"Not by the hair of my chinny-chin-chin!" shouted the third little pig.

"Then I'll huff, and I'll puff, and I'll BLOW your house in!" roared the wolf.

"We'll see about that," said the third little pig in his sturdy brick house.

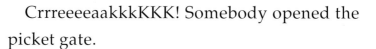

So the wolf huffed. And he huffed. But the red brick walls didn't even wiggle. Then he huffed and puffed. And PUFFED AND HUFFED—so hard all the buttons popped off his shirt. But the brick house didn't budge.

Then everything was quiet. VERY quiet.

The three little pigs sat down to enjoy their cinnamon tea. Then, they heard it…

SSSCCCCRRAAAAPE—claws on the roof!

"HELP!" squealed the second little pig. "He's coming down the chimney!"

"Stand back!" shouted the
third little pig. And quick as lightning
he hung the teapot over the fire.

WHOOOOSH. A bundle of gray fur slid
down the chimney.

PLOP! Cinnamon tea splashed everywhere.

"Weeeeeee-Owwww!" howled the wolf. And
his sharp, black claws carried him up the chimney
and over the picket fence, with cinnamon
tea dripping
from his long, gray tail
all along the way.

From that day to this, the Big Bad Wolf
has never been seen again.

And every night, the three little pigs
sleep safe and sound in the red brick
house—with the first little pig in his
bedroll, the second little pig in her
hammock, and the third little pig all cozy
and snug—in a room of his very own.

ABOUT THE AUTHOR

MARIAN HARRIS is not only an accomplished writer, but a former sheep farmer, copywriter, designer, kindergarten teacher, high school teacher, and college professor. She is author of several children's books, including *Goose and the Mountain Lion*—winner of the Colorado Book Award. Like *Goose and the Mountain Lion*, this book was a collaborative effort with her husband, Jim Harris, and of course their children.

ABOUT THE ILLUSTRATOR

JIM HARRIS is an accomplished illustrator whose first artistic triumph came in the fourth grade, when a tree he drew in art class was framed and displayed outside the principal's door. Over the years Jim's accomplishments have grown to include a host of diverse clients, from National Geographic to Sesame Street, and numerous awards, including the silver medal from New York's Society of Illustrators, Who's Who in the Midwest, and *Communication Arts'* Award for Illustration Excellence. Jim now spends most of his time illustrating children's books. He especially enjoys secretly re-creating his friends and family members as characters in books. His numerous children's books include the Reading Rainbow Book *The Three Little Javelinas.*

Today, Jim and Marian live with their three children at the end of a winding dirt road outside a remote mountain village in Colorado.